P9-DBW-897

BARNES SCHOOL LIBRARY

DISCARD

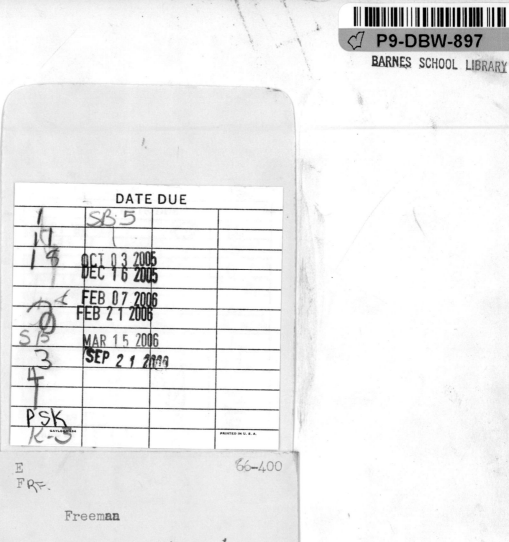

DATE DUE

	SB·5		
	OCT 0 3 2005		
	DEC 1 6 2005		
	FEB 07 2006		
	FEB 2 1 2006		
	MAR 1 5 2006		
	SEP 2 1 2000		

1
1
1
2
SB
3
4
PSK
R-5

GAYLORD 234   PRINTED IN U. S. A.

E
FRE.

66-400

Freeman

A rainbow of my own

A RAINBOW OF MY OWN

OF MY OWN

Don Freeman

The Viking Press   New York

66-400

BARNES SCHOOL LIBRARY

**To
David**

Copyright © 1966 by Don Freeman

All rights reserved

First published in 1966 by The Viking Press, Inc.
625 Madison Avenue, New York, N. Y. 10022

Published simultaneously in Canada by
The Macmillan Company of Canada Limited

Library of Congress catalog card number: 66-13983

Pic Bk

PRINTED IN THE U. S. A. BY REEHL LITHO., INC.

Today I saw a rainbow. It was so beautiful that I wanted to catch it for my very own.

I put on my raincoat and hat and ran outdoors.

Fast as the wind I ran.

But when I came to where the rainbow should have been,

it wasn't there.

I thought, Maybe some rainy day a rainbow will come and stay a while. I'll be walking along slowly,

and suddenly I'll hear a soft whirring sound
like the wings of a bird. I'll look around and see

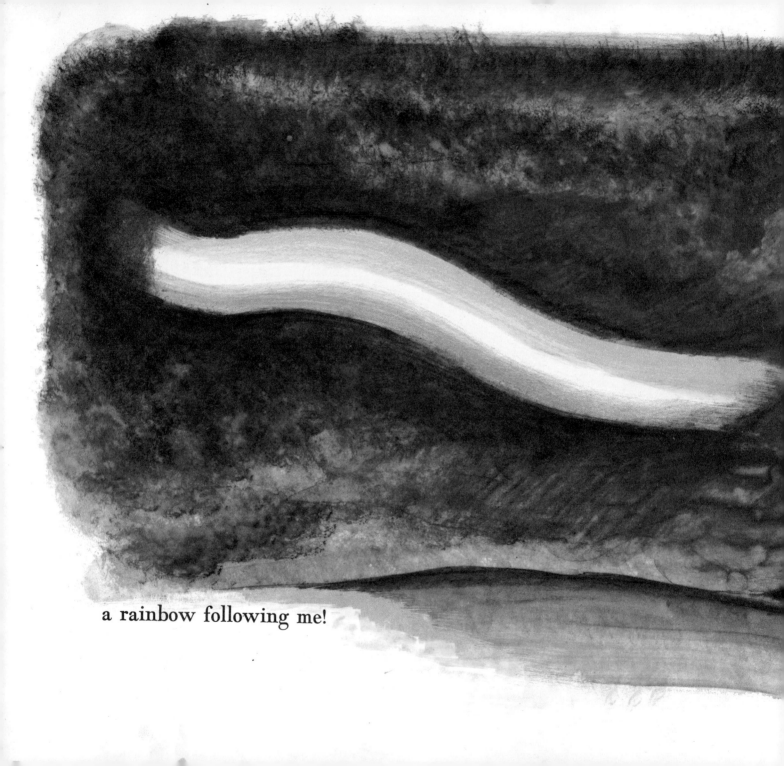

a rainbow following me!

I'll know by the way it circles and whirls

it wants to play.

So I'll hop over my rainbow,

and my rainbow will leap over me.

I'll climb up one side

and slide down the other.

My rainbow will make a peacock fan for me to walk in front of

and a hammock for me to swing in.

We'll play a game of hide-and-go-seek. I'll shut my eyes and count to twenty, and then look all around.

If I were a rainbow, where would I hide?

In a flower garden, of course!

Rows of flowers look like a rainbow.

BARNES SCHOOL LIBRARY

Suddenly the sun came out again from behind the rain clouds,

and my pretend rainbow disappeared the way real rainbows do.

But when I came back home, I saw something glowing
inside the window of my room,

and when I ran indoors,

there was a rainbow dancing on the wall! The sun was shining through the water in my goldfish bowl, and it made a rainbow just for me—

a rainbow of my very own!

BARNES SCHOOL LIBRARY

DISCARD